Filet of Soil

clay A readily molded earth used in making bricks and pottery

dirt Earth or soil

dust Fine particulate matter

grime Black dirt or soot

muck A moist mixture of mud

mud Wet, sticky, soft earth

slime A moist, sticky substance

slush Partially melted snow or ice

soil The upper most stratum of the earth's crust, especially the top few inches from which plants and ultimately man derive food

soot Black particles of carbon

tundra A treeless area of arctic regions

ISBN 0-9642206-3-6

Printed and published in the United States
by Windword Press.
Publisher is in Farmington Hills, MI 48334
(800) 718-5888

Library of Congress Catalog Card Number: 95-91036

This book was printed on
green paper.

For all the dirty,
soiled,
muddy,
slushy,
grimy,
mucky,
sooty,
dusty,
slimy,
things on the earth.

Nothing found
upon this earth
gets such
a dirty deal,
like that
which rests
beneath
our feet
that acts
just like
a peel.

It's plain just like
a crust of bread.

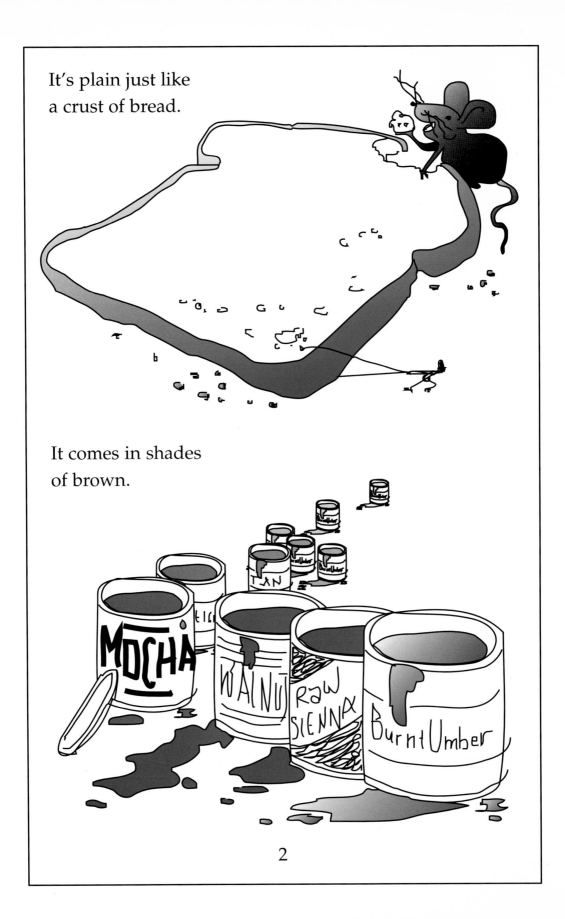

It comes in shades
of brown.

We never
give it
as a gift,

or find it
in a crown.

grime
MUD
SOOT tundra
SLUSH
DUST MUCK
SLIME
soil

It goes by many
names, indeed,
we take them all
for granted.

4

For every time
we mention it
our view is
fairly slanted.

5

But it is
nothing less
than earth
that stands
beneath
each foot.

We call it dust
within the air
that makes us
want to sneeze.

8

We call
it tundra
way up north
when it begins
to freeze.

9

We sometimes
call it grimy
if we get it
on our clothes.

We also
call it slimy
if it oozes
through our toes.

And if we glance
without delight,
it's called
a dirty look.

And if we read
what isn't nice
it's called
a dirty book.

We have
a dirty hand
if we cheat
while playing cards.

14

We have a dirty mouth
but never eat
the neighbors' yards.

These words
do not do justice.
They are worse
than dirty terms.

The ground
is like a palace
to those simple
things like worms.

It grows our grass,

our trees,

our shrubs,

our vegetables,

and flowers.

18

To those
whose feet
stay on
the ground,
it is
filet of soil.

It is the base
to buildings,

homes,

and neverending towers.

19

To every
creature
on our earth
it is
a source
of food.

Dirt is more
than just
a way
to say
unclean
or rude.

It is an anchor
for our feet
and what
we're meant
to be.

22

Instead of sky
for soaring wings,

and fins to swim
the sea.

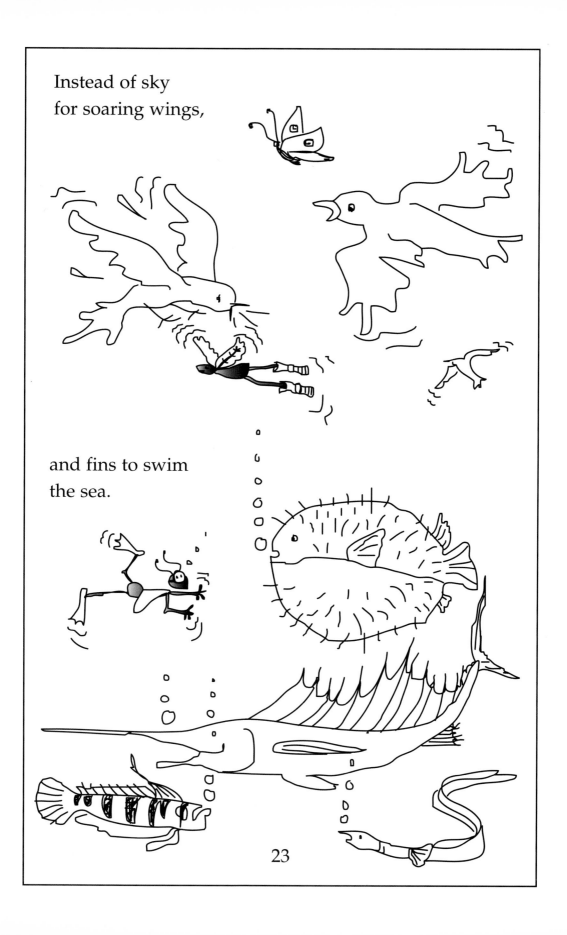

So dirt
may never
shine like gold,

or be considered
royal.

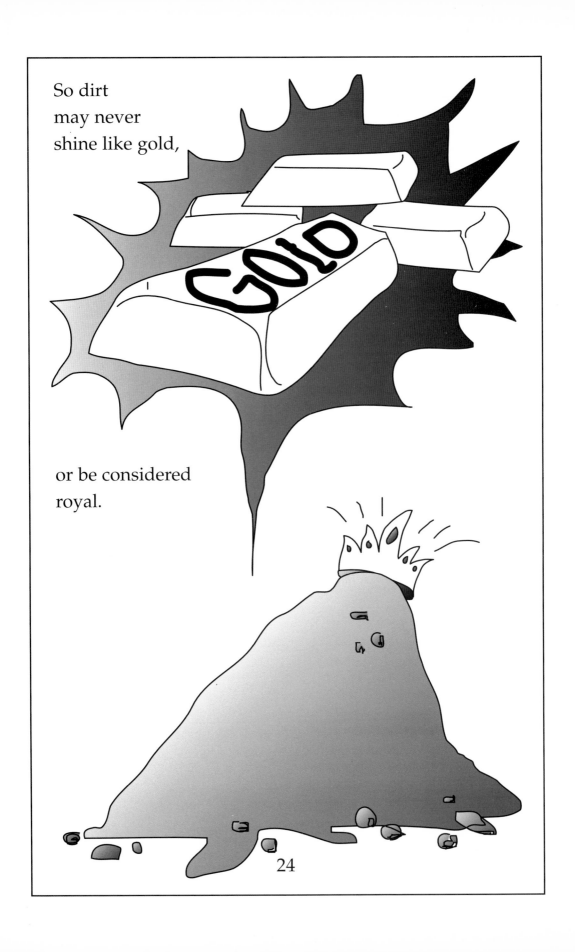

24

About the Author...
Barry Rudner lives in Keego Harbor, MI
basking in the wind, the water,
and the word.

About the Illustrator...
Peggy Trabalka lives, plays
and illustrates in Milford, MI.
She is a proud wife, mother,
and new grandmother.

About the Publisher...
Windword Press would like you to make two mud pies
before bed and call us in the morning.
You can tell us how you feel at
(800) 718-5888